MW00904463

STORY BY NEAL SWANSON
ART BY DANTE BANUELOS

WWW.BRINGCUTENESSBACK.COM

The Atomic Dogs and the distinctive logo, character design, and concept are registered trademarks of Delorean, Brown & McFly.
Story & Concept by Neal Swanson | Illustrations by Dante Banuelos
Text & illustration copyright © 2018 by Delorean, Brown & McFly| ISBN# 978-0997138856

All rights reserved. No part of this publication may be reproduced, stored in a retrieval system, or transmitted in any form or by any means, electronic, mechanical, photocopying, recording or otherwise, without prior permission of the publisher and copyright owner. First printing published by: Wear Cupcakes, LLC dba Delorean, Brown & McFly. For more information about custom editions, special sales, wholesaling, and premium and corporate purchases, please contact the sales department at 360-510-3325 or smile@bringcutenessback.com.

THIS BOOK IS DEDICATED TO ALL THE RESCUE DOGS WE'VE BEEN LUCKY ENOUGH TO CALL A PART OF OUR FAMILY OVER THE YEARS. THANK YOU FOR PROVIDING ENDLESS ENTERTAINMENT, FRIENDSHIP, LOVE, AND A CONSTANT REMINDER OF WHAT MATTERS MOST.

LOVE,
THE SWANSONS

ON AN ORDINARY STREET IN AN ORDINARY TOWN LIVED AN ORDINARY FAMILY WITH THREE EXTRA ORDINARY DOGS.

THE OLDEST OF THE THREE DOGS WAS NAMED CHARLIE. HE HAD SOFT BLACK FUR AND LEGS THAT WERE JUST A LITTLE TOO SHORT FOR HIS BODY.

SOMETIMES CHARLIE WOULD SEARCH FOR TREATS THE FAMILY MAY HAVE LEFT OUT WHEN THEY WERE GONE DURING THE DAY.

SOON AFTER, CHARLIE BEGAN TO CHANGE!

HE COULD HEAR BETTER!

HE COULD SEE CLEARER!

HE COULD EVEN RUN FASTER!

CHARLIE CALLED OVER DUKE AND HOPE, THE OTHER TWO DOGS IN THE HOUSE, AND TOLD THEM WHAT HAPPENED. HE GAVE THEM EACH A COOKIE TO TRY FOR THEMSELVES AND WITHIN SECONDS THEY BEGAN TO CHANGE TOO.

THE THIRD DOG IN THE HOUSE WAS NAMED DUKE. HE WAS A BIG YELLOW DOG THAT ATE EVERYTHING HE COULD GET HIS PAWS ON. EVEN THOUGH HE WAS EXTRA LARGE, THE ATOMIC DOG COOKIES WORKED ON HIM AS WELL.

EACH TIME THE DOGS ATE AN ATOMIC DOG COOKIE, THEY WOULD TRANSFORM INTO THEIR SUPER-DOG ALTER EGOS AND COMBINE THEIR POWERS TO BECOME:

THE ATOMIC DOGS

THEY TRAINED OFTEN, CONVINCED THAT WITHOUT SUPER-DOG PROTECTION, THEIR HOME WOULD FALL VICTIM TO THE SUPER VILLIANS THEY HAD MET IN THE NEIGHBORHOOD OVER THE YEARS. SUCH AS...

THE MAD MAILMAN

THE CLEVER CAT

THE ARMY OF SQUIRRELS

UNFORTUNATELY FOR THE ATOMIC DOGS, EACH TIME THEY ATE A COOKIE, THEIR POWERS WERE ONLY TEMPORARY.

AS THE EFFECTS OF THE COOKIES WORE OFF, THE ATOMIC DOGS ALWAYS RETURNED TO THEIR CLUMSY, SCARED, AND SILLY OLD SELVES.

THE ATOMIC DOGS DID THEIR BEST TO PROTECT THEIR HOME EACH DAY WHILE THEIR FAMILY WAS AWAY.

THEY KNEW IF THEY WORKED TOGETHER THEY COULD ACCOMPLISH ANYTHING, OR SO THEY THOUGHT...

IT WAS A SUNNY SUMMER DAY AT THE HOME OF THE ATOMIC DOGS. CHARLIE WAS NAPPING ON THE COUCH AND HOPE WAS ASLEEP ON THE BED.

MEANWHILE, DUKE WAS ON HIS DAILY PATROL OF THE BACKYARD WHEN HE HEARD SOMETHING IN THE BUSHES. HE BEGAN TO BARK LOUDLY AND RAN INSIDE TO TELL THE OTHERS WHAT HE HAD SEEN.

CHARLIE BARKED OUT HIS ORDERS, "EACH OF YOU EAT AN ATOMIC DOG COOKIE, WE HAVE NO TIME TO SPARE!"

DUKE STOOD TALL AS THE SUPER POWERED COOKIE MADE HIS JAW AS STRONG AS A LION AND HIS FUR INTO BODY ARMOR AS STRONG AS STEEL.

As the others made their transformation, Charlie rolled over in the speed of light and emerged as

KUNG FU CHARLIE

The supreme leader of the atomic dogs.

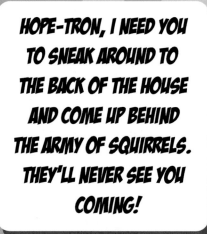
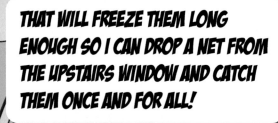

KUNG FU CHARLIE WATCHED AS DUKE WAS STUCK IN THE BACK DOOR, HOPE WAS TRAPPED UNDER A NET, AND WORST OF ALL, THE SQUIRRELS WERE GETTING AWAY YET AGAIN.

As the dog's super powers wore off, Duke found a way out of the back door, and Hope finally escaped the net.

Soon after, their family returned home and the three dogs wagged their tails with excitement, proud to have kept the squirrels away for one more day!

THE ATOMIC DOGS LIVED IN A NEIGHBORHOOD WITH ONLY ONE MAILMAN. HE WAS TALL, HE WAS SKINNY, AND HE ...
HATED DOGS!

AROUND THE SAME TIME EACH DAY, THE MAILMAN WOULD WALK UP TO THE HOME OF THE ATOMIC DOGS AND SLIDE THE MAIL THROUGH A SLOT IN THE FRONT DOOR.

INSIDE THE HOUSE, THE SMALLEST OF THE ATOMIC DOGS, CHARLIE, WOULD ATTACK THE MAIL AS IT PASSED THROUGH THE SLOT, BITING AND TEARING INTO IT UNTIL IT REMAINED IN A PILE OF PIECES ON THE FLOOR.

WHILE CHARLIE DESTROYED THE MAIL, THE LARGEST OF THE ATOMIC DOGS, DUKE, WOULD BARK AS LOUD AS HE COULD TO SCARE THE MAILMAN AWAY.

AS THE MAILMAN RAN AWAY HE WOULDALWAYS YELL OUT...
I'LL GET YOU DOGS SOMEDAY!

OVER THE YEARS, THE MAILMAN TRIED TO GET BACK AT THE DOGS, BUT WITH EACH FAILED ATTEMPT HE GREW ANGRIER AND ANGRIER. EVENTUALLY, HE BECAME ONE OF THE ATOMIC DOGS GREATEST FOES...

THE MAD MAILMAN!

ONE DAY, DUKE WAS BUSY SNIFFING FLOWERS IN THE BACKYARD AT THE SAME TIME THE MAD MAILMAN STOPPED HIS TRUCK TO GET READY TO DELIVER THE MAIL.

DUKE LISTENED TO THE MAD MAILMAN TALKING TO HIMSELF AS HE BEGAN TO FILL HIS BAG WITH MAIL, "THESE DOGS HAVE NO IDEA WHAT I HAVE IN STORE FOR THEM THIS TIME, HA, HA, HA!"

DUKE WAS CURIOUS, SO HE LOOKED THROUGH A HOLE IN THE FENCE AS THE MAD MAILMAN CONTINUED, "THESE TRIPLE STRENGTH FART-BOMB DOG COOKIES I WHIPPED UP ARE SURE TO RUIN THEIR DAY. I'LL PUT SOME IN AN ENVELOPE AND SLIP IT IN WITH THE REST OF THE MAIL. WHEN THOSE FUR BALLS TEAR INTO IT THEY'LL BE FARTING FOR THE REST OF THE DAY,

"HA, HA, HA!"

THE MAD MAILMAN SLIPPED THE ENVELOPE LOADED WITH TRIPLE STRENGTH FART-BOMB DOG COOKIES INTO HIS BAG AND HEADED FOR THE FRONT DOOR OF THE ATOMIC DOGS.

DUKE WOBBLED INSIDE THE HOUSE TO WARN THE OTHERS OF WHAT WAS COMING BEFORE THE MAD MAILMAN HAD A CHANCE TO DELIVER HIS POSTAL PUNISHMENT.

HE THREE DOGS QUICKLY SWALLOWED THEIR COOKIES JUST AS THE MAD MAILMAN APPEARED AT THE FRONT DOOR.

AS THE MAD MAILMAN STOOD FROZEN IN PLACE, KUNG FU CHARLIE HANDED THE FART-BOMB COOKIES TO HOPE-TRON WHO LAUNCHED HERSELF INTO THE AIR.

SHE FLEW OUT OF THE DOOR AND THREW ALL OF THEM DIRECTLY INTO THE MAD MAILMAN'S WIDE OPEN MOUTH.

ALL THREE DOGS LAUGHED AS THEY WATCHED THE MAD MAILMAN RUN BACK TO HIS TRUCK WITH ONE HAND ON HIS BUM AND MAIL FLYING EVERYWHERE. "HE WON'T BE MESSING WITH US ANYTIME SOON", HOPE-TRON LAUGHED.

STORY BY NEAL SWANSON
ART BY DANTE BANUELOS

EACH MORNING, THE ATOMIC DOGS WENT FOR A LONG WALK IN THEIR NEIGHBORHOOD.

THEY WOULD WAG THEIR TAILS AND SAY HELLO TO THE NEIGHBORS AS THEY SNIFFED THE FLOWERS ALONG THE WAY.

THE ATOMIC DOGS NICKNAMED HIM THE CLEVER CAT AND THEY HAD BEEN SWORN ENEMIES EVER SINCE.

THE DOGS MADE IT BACK IN RECORD TIME AND FOUND THEIR FAVORITE SPOTS TO TAKE AN AFTERNOON NAP, HAPPY TO BE HOME SAFE AND SOUND.

IT WAS THE CLEVER CAT! HE WAS FIRING PINECONES LIKE MISSILES AT CHARLIE FROM THE TREE TOPS.

CHARLIE HAD TO GET BACK INSIDE TO WARN THE OTHERS, THE CLEVER CAT WAS ON THE ATTACK!

THE DOGS GOT INTO POSITION UNDER HOPE'S BLANKET AND SLOWLY CREPT INTO THE BACKYARD.

THE CLEVER CAT IMMEDIATELY BEGAN TO FIRE PINECONES AT THE DOGS LIKE MISSILES, PING, POW, ZING!

THE CAT WAS HIT SO MANY TIMES HE LOST HIS BALANCE AND DROPPED THE REST OF THE PINECONE MISSILES.

THE ATOMIC DOGS STORY IS BASED ON THREE REAL LIFE RESCUE DOGS NAMED CHARLIE, HOPE, AND DUKE. PLEASE REMEMBER TO SUPPORT YOUR LOCAL SHELTER OR RESCUE ORGANIZATION WHERE THERE ARE ALWAYS AMAZING ANIMALS LOOKING FOR LOVING HOMES.

55307506R00055

Made in the USA
San Bernardino, CA
31 October 2017